Sam's Jam For Gran

Written and illustrated by Catherine Brockhurst

Sam's Gran was poorly.

Sam knew she was poorly, because whenever he asked to visit her, his Mum looked worried and Dad tried to change the subject, for no reason. Also, Sam heard his auntie Kate whispering about a hospital, the cost of parking and 'the disgusting mashed potato and gravy, that mum moaned about every day'. Sam knew something must be wrong with Gran, because she hated gravy, she'd never stick around for that unless she had to.

Gran said gravy was gross, what
Sam's Gran really loved
was jam,

Gran was the world's biggest
jam fan.

Ever.

Gran had jam on toast for breakfast, in her sandwiches for lunch, and she'd always choose jam roly-polly when they went out for Sunday lunch. And for her birthdays she always asked for a jam sponge cake. She really, really, really LOVED jam.

Sam missed his Gran, they watched cooking shows together after school, and quizzes and even cartoons about superheroes if Sam was lucky, and they'd make toasted tea cakes or scones with jam, to eat while they watched.

After hearing what Gran had said about the gravy, Sam was worried there wouldn't be jam for Gran at the hospital, that she'd be stuck with gross gravy. So Sam hatched a plan. He'd make her some jam and smuggle it in to her when his Mum and Dad took him to visit.

He'd need some tools for his jam plan, he'd need a squisher for the fruit, a giant bowl because he'd have to make a lot of the stuff, especially if Gran was going to be in hospital for a while, one jar wouldn't be enough, not with the way Gran ate jam.

Hmm - a jam squisher. He thought hard, what could he use...? He'd seen a tv show one time where the lady was squishing grapes in a big bucket with her feet...He could try that...

If he was going to do all that stomping with his feet he was going to have to get a pretty big bucket - hmm thought Sam. A big bucket. Ooh, how about the bath?! Excellent idea.

Gran's favourite jam was strawberry, but Sam was worried there wouldn't be enough of those in the fridge, maybe he could squish up a mixed fruit jam? Sam searched through the fridge and kitchen cupboards and found strawberries, bananas, tinned peaches and pears, grapes, and raspberries. He was pretty sure jam had lots of sugar in it too. He'd heard Mum say Gran would rot her teeth with all the jam she ate. Gran had just laughed and tapped her teeth like a front door 'bit late for that Jane', she'd said, chuckling.

Sam really missed his Gran.

Sam carried all the fruit into the bathroom. He'd also grabbed a bag of sugar while he'd been in the kitchen. Next, he tipped the sugar and all the fruit in the bath. He took his socks off, examined them for fluff...And had a sniff for stinkiness, they seemed ok...So Sam jumped in.

At first it was hard going, the fruit didn't squish all that easily and the sugar felt very gritty between Sam's toes, but once the bananas and strawberries softened it started to get pretty gooey. When the rest of the fruit caught up, it was a slushy, sloppy mess and looked JUST LIKE JAM!

Sam climbed out of the bath. It was a very messy job, there was Sam's jam all over the taps, bath, towels and floor. Never mind, thought Sam, it would be worth it when Gran got her jam.

But he still had the problem of where to store his awesome jam. He'd need to smuggle it into the hospital. I wonder...thought Sam...Could that work? Only a couple of months ago, Gran had given Sam some birthday money and Sam had invested in two super, high powered, pump action water pistols...If that worked it would be PERFECT! He'd use the excuse of wanting to show Gran how he'd spent her gift. Sam snuck into his room and grabbed the water pistols. It was heavy going filling them up. Jam was a very messy business. But before long Sam had two primed Jam pistols ready to go. He got to work cleaning up his mess and now to be patient until it was time to visit.

Sure enough, Sam didn't have to wait long, the next day his mum sat him down and explained that Gran was poorly, and in hospital until she was better. But that she was very much up for a visit, so they'd be heading to the hospital THAT AFTERNOON! Sam asked to take his water pistols to show Gran (he asked in a light and airy way, the way dad did about watching all day cricket) and mum did not suspect a thing.

The car journey to the hospital was a bit hairy, Sam had to keep the pistols upright to stop them dripping his delicious jam everywhere, each bump in the road felt like he was driving over a cliff! Sam held tight.

When they got to the hospital it still wasn't plain sailing, Sam had never seen anywhere so white and clean, no place for sticky jam, he thought. But he kept his cool as they traveled through corridor after corridor.

Until finally...GRAN!! Sam ran to his Gran's bed and gave her the biggest hug and she gave him an even bigger hug back.

Gran definitely looked like she could do with a giant helping of jam, so while Mum was busy talking to the nurse, Sam whispered his jam plan to Gran. Sam's Gran whooped with delight! 'What is it mum?!' Cried Sam's mum. 'Ooh I'm just so HUNGRY Jane, could I have some bread and butter, some crackers, some toast and a bowl of porridge please?!'. 'Erm, I should think so Mum, let me go and ask'. Off went Sam's Mum to track down food for Gran, feeling very cheered that she felt like eating again.

While Sam's mum was out of the way it gave Sam time to get his jam pistols ready. Gran held them by her sides just out of sight, ready to smother her food in Sam's delicious jam.

Mum came back in, and she had a great big tray, covered in toast, porridge, and crackers. She set it down on the table in front of gran. 'Bingo' shouted gran, pulling the jam pistols out from beneath the covers. 'READY AIM FIRE' she shouted. And then...?! JAAAAAAM EVERYWHERE!

There was jam on the toast, jam on the porridge, jam on the crackers, jam on the walls, jam on the ceiling, the fan, the windows AND the doctors and nurses doing their rounds. Jam on mum, jam on Sam. And Gran?

Gran had the biggest jammy smile on her face Sam had ever seen, a big jammy smile full of a big slice of jammy toast.

Well, after mum had apologised to all the staff and Gran had stopped grinning and eating and had agreed to give the pistols back, and the porters and Mum and Sam had cleaned up, Gran pulled him in for another hug.

'That, Sam my boy, was the best jam I have EVER tasted' she whispered. 'When I get out of here, we're going to make a hundred new batches of Sam's Jam. But in the meantime let's keep quiet about my little reserve ok'? And Gran showed Sam a little pill pot of his jam she'd snuck behind her water jug. 'Genius, Gran', said Sam.

He gave her a another huge sticky hug and promised her he'd be back soon...

With LOTS more jam!

Sam's Jam For Gran started as a story for my little boy Tom, who, like Sam, is a massive fan of gigantic monster water pistols, his fun on sunny days inspired this story. He's also not so little now, but still loves story time - you're never too old for a story.

For my husband Mark and my boy, Tom; I love you.

And thanks too to my parents, Sue and Luke and my brothers; Jesse, Jake and Sean

Keep an eye out for more adventures for Sam and his Gran…

Catherine Brockhurst is an artist and illustrator living on the south coast of England with her husband, son and menagerie – including a super friendly pup, two cats and a surprisingly speedy tortoise named Groot.

Printed in Great Britain
by Amazon

76753783R00016